The Berenstain Bears®
and the

TALENT SHOW

Stan & Jan
Berenstain

A GOLDEN BOOK • NEW YORK
Western Publishing Company, Inc., Racine, Wisconsin 53404

At Bear Country School
early one spring,
a call was put out
for cubs who could sing,

TALENT CALL:
SINGERS
DANCERS
MUSICIANS
JUGGLERS
ETC.

for cubs who could dance—
tap or soft-shoe,

for cubs who could play
a horn or kazoo,

3

for cubs who could juggle
three balls in the air…

Then a special call went out
for Brother Bear.

BROTHER BEAR, PLEASE REPORT TO MISS SMITH.

5

"I called on you
because, as you know,
I am in charge of
the talent show."

"Miss Smith, I'd be happy
to help with the show.
But I have no talent—
as far as I know."

6

"You may have some talent
you don't know about.
But what I need now
is a *talent scout*."

"If a talent scout
is what you need,
I'll be happy to help,"
Brother agreed.

So Brother scouted Sister,
who could dance on her toes,

and Fred, who could balance
a pole on his nose.

Barry was able
to make his ears wiggle.
Those ears were always
good for a giggle.

Brother's friend Bill
could do clever tricks.

Black Belt Bertha
could smash through bricks.

Queenie McBear

could do a back flip.

"My talent," said Too-Tall,
"is my powerful grip."

"Er, a grip isn't quite
what we had in mind.
Please try something else,
if you'd be so kind."

"Not enough," said Miss Smith
when she saw Brother's list.
"There must be some talented cubs
that you missed."

So talent scout Brother
kept scouting around.

Here are some more
of the talents he found.

A cub who could tell
the funniest jokes.

HA!
HA
HA!
HA

A cub who could imitate
famous folks.

A cub who had

a ventriloquist's dummy.

One who patted his head
while rubbing his tummy.

A cub who pulled rabbits
out of top hats.

A group of cubs
who were acrobats.

Uh-oh! Here's Too-Tall
for another try.
Look at the fire
in his eye!

This time he's brought
his whole gang along.
"This time," he said,
"I will sing you a song!"

Too-Tall's talent
was a big surprise.
You could see the surprise
in Brother Bear's eyes.

"Hey, Too-Tall!
Way to go!
That was great!
You're in the show!"

And what a talent show
it was!
The bears of Bear Country
were all abuzz!

There were
funny jokes,

HA!
HA!
HA!
HA!

imitations of
famous folks,

CLAP!
CLAP!
CLAP!

Sister Bear dancing
on her toes,

Fred with a pole
on the tip of his nose,

rabbits from hats,

and acrobats,

clever tricks,

and broken bricks.

But Too-Tall's talent
was surely the best.

A little bit better
than all the rest.

"One moment, please.
Before you go,
let's thank all the cubs
who were in our show…

and one special cub,
whom I'm sure you all know.
Without *his* talent,
there would *be* no show.

It's Brother Bear,
our talent scout—
a talent we could not
have done without."

The applause for Brother
was long and loud.
"Thank you," said Brother.
He was very proud.